Pages from the Heart

By

Elizabeth B. Bouladian

Pages from the Heart

Poems By

Elizabeth B. Bouladian

Copyright © 2009 by Elizabeth B. Bouladian

Pages From The Heart
by Elizabeth B. Bouladian

Printed in the United States of America

ISBN 978-1-60791-468-6

All rights reserved solely by the author. The author guarantees all contents are original and do not infringe upon the legal rights of any other person or work. No part of this book may be reproduced in any form without the permission of the author. The views expressed in this book are not necessarily those of the publisher.

www.xulonpress.com

Dearborn Heights, Michigan
Jan 13, 2010

Dear Dr. Henry:
With best wishes
Elizabeth Baran Bouladian

Contents

1. A conversation with my mother I 9
2. A conversation with my mother II 10
3. The first day of kindergarten 11
4. The first Christmas at school 12
5. The first Christmas at home 13
6. The first Sunday 14
7. The wedding crowds 15
8. Quiet time... 16
9. My sister... 17
10. My brother 18
11. My big brother 20
12. Mugsy 22
13. Learning to swim 24
14. Freedom 25
15. Ode to Aleppo 27
16. The red sweater 28
17. The windowsill.. 29
18. Mother of mine 30
19. A night in the bomb shelter 31
20. Eternal poison 33
21. The sahara of the soul 34
22. In the wilderness 35
23. The old remedy 36
24. Big Gretta.. 38
25. What's on your mind?.. 39

26. The color of the tide 40
27. Remember me when I die 41
28. Carrying on 42
29. Rosa 43
30. Spring always comes 44
31. Come get bored with me 45
32. The expert 46
33. Labels 47
34. The Book and a sewing machine 50
35. Night-Sky Flyer 52
36. Ara (In Memoriam) 54
37. The Falafel Shop 56
38. Disappointments 58
39. The Bug 59
40. Let it take its course 60
41. Celebration of Armenian Tradition 61
42. Jano 63
43. The prodigal daughter 64
44. Honey's honey 65
45. Where am I from? 66
46. The Ripple Prayer 67

A conversation with my mother
I

If you behave well,
while I am giving you your bath,
Baba will bring mshabbak* tonight
You love it, don't you?
I couldn't answer because I could not speak
But I certainly understood.
I must have behaved well and did not cry
despite the ghar** soap burning my eyes.
This is the only recollection I have of my father
That he was going to bring mshabbak that night
If I behaved.

*Mshabbak is a Middle-Eastern Pastry.
**Ghar soap is made of olive oil.

A conversation with my mother
II

Light your candles by his grave
Make a groove in the stones,
and put your incense there
Protect the candles by a piece of cardboard
and another piece of discarded tin
But please don't cry
Mother: my heart is bleeding over you
Mother: you're making me cry too
I don't know why I'm crying
Let us take the bus and go home
My brothers and sisters will cheer us up
Oh mother I am here for you
I'll always be there for you
I'm speaking to you in the language of tears
Your loud lamenting is breaking my heart
A candle gets blown out
It is a windy day in Aleppo
Oh, please let us take the bus
and go home
Where there is life.

The first day of kindergarten

Your sisters will be with you
You'll see. School is nice!
I got on the jungle gym
Soon a bell rang
The children lined up
I looked around in panic
Oh! Where are my sisters?
My sisters have abandoned me too.
Come on, cajoled Miss Sarah
Let's go into class
It'll be fun.
I can't remember how
But somehow I made it through
the first day of school.

The first Christmas at school

Make way! I have to get home!
I have to show mother what Santa brought me.
He really liked me.
I had my arms full of packages
Mama and my brothers
Had made sure I'd get the most gifts.
I stumbled on the way home
but didn't let anybody help me carry the gifts
They were mine
The world was mine.

The first Christmas at home

I had a mandarin orange
I stuck a blue candle in it
Soon I'll get to light it
Mother sat down
All her children were sitting around her
For some reason she seemed happy
We had our Christmas dinner
But soon the boys left
Mama and us girls were left alone
Where did the boys go? I pondered
But did not ask.
They were going to play with other friends
I guessed.
Ooh, what fun was I missing?

The first Sunday

Ha-Hallelujah
Went the song
I sang with all my heart
I had a quarter
I put it in the basket.
A girl did not have any money
She took a handful from the basket
and put it back with a jingle.
No! Said the minister's son
This is real Church
You have to put real money.
I was amazed
Where do all these quarters go anyway?
I pondered
But did not ask.
After Sunday school
A bus took everyone home
Our house faced the Church
But I got on the bus anyway
We went around the city
letting off children at their houses
When we returned to Church
We would chant
Here we are back to Church
Here we are back at home.

The wedding crowds

Our neighbor, Mrs. Lucia, took me to all the weddings
In the neighboring Churches in old Aleppo
And there were lots of Churches
Mostly we did not know the people
Of course we did not know the bride and the groom
But we went anyway to see the Church service
To look at the bride's gown
And check out everything.
We went from Church to Church
usually on Saturday afternoons.

Mrs. Lucia told me very seriously,
Where have you been?
I tearfully replied that I got lost in the crowd
Mrs. Lucia put her old and cold hand in mine
And off we went to another wedding.
I did not know at that time that life would be
A series of weddings
that I would not be able to attend
And that it wasn't the last time
I would be lost in a crowd.

Quiet time

Mrs. Lucia and I
Sat in the large room
I sat by the door to the balcony
on a wicker chair
She sat on the sofa
a tiny table in front of her
playing solitaire
with an old deck of cards.

The clock kept going tick tok, tick tok
I watched the merchants on the street close their shutters
One by one they left for the evening.
The jeweler, the carpenter and the ice cream maker.
I waited for Mrs. Lucia to say something
Tick tok, tick tok

Her red hair was gleaming in the setting sun
the shuffle of the cards went scuff scuff
Mrs. Lucia was silent
Only the clock was going in that room
tick tok, tick tok.
She gave me two stale biscuits
Then mom came knocking on the door.
How was work? Asked Mrs. Lucia,
Mother spoke to her briefly
as she ushered me out
To take me home.

My sister

Mother called her
"Little Mom"
She sewed dresses for my doll
She cooked meals
in the summer.
She was the apple of mom's eye
And I loved her too.

She bathed me
She convinced me
that my long hair
needed to be washed four times
Once, she said, to "wet it"
Twice to clean it
And once with a fancy shampoo, which she made up
by jiggling the ghar soap
in a tiny amount of warm water
making lots and lots of lather
In a little container
that she used to pour water on me.
And I would feel pampered like a queen.
Nobody gets away with soapy water for shampoo
except my sister
She convinced me that it was
the best shampoo in the world.

I watched her grow up
I watched her crowned May Queen
I watched her fall in love,
Marry,
And become a real mom.

My brother

The "King of cute"
If I have ever seen one

"Get me a cup of water
Or I'll die"
He would slowly bend his head onto his chest
I would race to the kitchen
And rush back to save him
from certain death.

Whenever "King of cute"
wanted a favor
he counted to ten
so I would oblige
Or he would die

Soon I learned that
I could take my time
I could even have a snack
And that all would still be well

"Little girl you look sad
I'll take you to the park"
He bought me ice cream,
and a soft drink
He even had a freelance photographer
take our picture
In Aleppo's biggest park.
I still have the picture.

I could always depend on him
to cheer me up
All he had to do
was show up
And the sadness would vanish
Like magic
It is still that way
Whenever the "King of cute" calls
from far away
My clouds are scattered
In the time it takes
to count to ten.

My big brother

The teacher is absent today
Other teachers will fill in
Teachers came and teachers went
throughout the day

In comes my brother
He's a teacher now
I better behave, I thought,
But then I reminded myself that
I always behaved well
When he was around.
Unlike Mugsy,
this brother was very strict
He did not put up
With girlish chatter and giggles

I am going to make him
proud of me
I raised my hand to solve an addition problem
on the blackboard.

The blackboard was high
I was tiny
With all the dignity that a child could muster
I climbed on the wooden bench
placed for us to reach the board
then
to my big embarassment
down I fell
to the floor
bench and all

My big brother raced towards me
He made sure I was all right
He still does that
I still try my best to impress him.

Mugsy

I'll draw you a picture
of the house fly

It was the first time
Mugsy offered to do my homework

I looked at the beautiful fly
Sketched in pencil
on a full page
I knew my teacher
would never believe
that it was I
who sketched the shaded house fly

I do not recall
how I submitted my homework
But all went well,
somehow

Mugsy took me to
his class's Christmas party
At his school

All the children
sat behind their desks
which were put in a large circle

There was music
there were treats
I was proud to be
his sister
I was happy to be
his sister
He knew how to treat
a little girl well.

Learning to swim

Splash!
My brother threw me into the swimming pool
I was floating in an inner tube
but scared to death
I began crying
Then I started wiggling my arms and legs
He jumped to my side
I calmed down

My brother and one of his friends
trained me to swim a few meters
Between their outstretched arms
In a few days
the tube was gone
I was swimming on my own
and never left the pool
until it was time to go home.

Freedom

I can read!
I can read!
I told my sister
but she didn't show much cheer
She could already read
But I was full of glee
I could read my textbooks
Without much effort
I finished half the stories in my reading book
the first day
The other half the next day.

A story about a mother
and daughter
saddened me
My eyes welled with tears
I started loving my mother even more
Mother noticed that I could read
She flooded me with children's books
I was Cinderella one day
Joan of Arc the next
I went to India or America
by the flip of a page
My horizon expanded
I read my sister's books
I read to enjoy
I read to remember
I read to grow
I didn't have to ask questions anymore
I just read the answers.

continued

To read is to live
over and over
To read
is to be free
Good bye childhood
I can now read.

Ode to Aleppo

Valley of good people
Wise and frugal
Kind and simply noble
Almost regal.

Castle of the tough
Gated city
Always welcoming
Supporting those who struggle
on their way to reach higher
and still higher

City of many gates
Guarded by angels
and the remains of saints
Offering relaxed days
Deep siestas
Lazy strolls
and calm quiet nights
of childhood slumber.

The red sweater

She knitted it with love
for her betrothed
The engagement broke off
But his mother kept the red sweater
in a chest
Never worn

War times came
The mother retrieved the red sweater from its box
She undid the threads so lovingly knit
Her daughters rolled the threads on their young arms
They washed the threads to give them new luster
They hung the wool clusters to dry
on a clothes line in an eastern window
They knit the wool
into a new sweater

The girls shared the love sweater
Until someone stole it
The red sweater may have gone
But the love put in every stitch
lingered on
In the hearts of the young lovers
In the dreams of the young girls
In the prayers of the mother
Blessing her son and his beloved
Love bloomed despite the war
Despite the hard times
Love was true to itself.

The windowsill

Like a drama unfolding
Mama walked sister to work
in the mornings
Under shelling and sniper fire
and waited for her to come home in the afternoon
At the ever patient witness
Our windowsill

Twenty-five cars have passed
Gunfire erupted
Yet there was no sign
Of the large car
bringing my sister back home

"Don't murmur that sad song!
Sing something cheerful"
Said my mother

At the windowsill
every evening we would wait
praying for my sister
to make it home safely

Hurried footsteps are heard
breaking the silence in the street
I lean hard on the sill
It is sister
I run to open the door
Mama stays by the window
The drama ends for that day.

Mother of mine

I saw you as a beauty
when you were forty

At forty-one, I reminisce,
You looked remote and cloudy

Years passed, I never stopped admiring
the art work you created in every meal
In every stitch of the needle
In every lesson you taught me
about the nature of things
and people.

Years passed, but you remained steadfast
In nurturing
In teaching
In sacrificing
With all humility
You taught me the meaning of
Loyalty

Mother and daughter
We learned about each other
We closed the doors to sorrow
We sang about love
About a sunny tomorrow
Mother of mine
Even in the autumn of your years
You showed me how to be a hero.

A night in the bomb shelter

I am going to the "night club"
Bombing escalated around sunset
I wouldn't hear the crashing sounds
three floors underground
in the shelter
I called the nightclub

I took a bottle of water
put on some perfume to cheer up
Bid my mom good night
And before the bombing started
I headed to the nightclub

Hi Armig
Hi Aida
Hi Mrs. Perouz
Hi Mr. Tertsagian
Hi Silva

Armig had put on a ton of make up
Aida was discussing politics
Mrs. Perouz was sleeping in her chair
Mr. Tertsagian was singing a French song
Silva had just had plastic surgery on her nose.

continued

People started coming to the nightclub
any time after six
At eight the club was full.
Some played solitaire
Some played cards in groups of four
Mrs. Perouz snored, shook, and woke up for a minute
She clutched more firmly the purse,
which we all knew,
contained all her jewelry,
then she went back to sleep
in the uncomfortable chair

Lights went out at eleven at night
Those who were playing solitaire blew out their candles
Card players scattered to their cots
Radios were turned off
Perouz woke up
to face a long night.

Eternal poison

The sweet poison
attracted me
I gasped, choked and died for two decades
I woke up by myself and very alone
There was no kiss from prince charming
Alchemy did its magic
And I woke up on my own.

The Sahara of the Soul

The pain was unbearable and numbing,
Body and soul felt dead.
"Friends" shook their heads and vanished
Never to return
They could see I was dead.
My family did not bury me.
They could not accept that I was dead
This cannot be the end.
Like a vegetable they watered and fed me
Praying and hoping.
People talked of life and of the living
I no longer understood life or the living
How could I understand with no senses?
My soul's eyes saw only darkness, deep and infinite
The involuntary functions such as heart beat
and breathing
continued
Though the spirit lost its desire for life.

In the wilderness

It used to be blue
There was an azure horizon
I parked the car
On the sands of the Mediterranean
Sand everywhere I only saw.

What happened here?
There were trees on the shore
We used to smell beauty off the sea
There were magnificent waves in the winter
The wind played its notes in the summer
What happened here?

I implored the sky for an answer
Angry clouds looked down
A dry wind blew
Sand got in my eyes
The kindest Book
was quoted by people
Only to generate further sand
Infinite sand on the shores of my heart.

The old remedy

I am King Lear
And I am his clown
I gave my reins to others
And regretted every word uttered

I'll tell you more
About people white, black, and brown
Who've crossed my path
And made me regret
The day I was born
I too, took their sins
Piled them on mine
And hanged myself
On a crazy day's dawn

I was left hanging
Long after sun down
Until a merciful Arimathean
Took me down
I was wrapped in a scarlet gown
Put in a box
And shipped somewhere forlorn
Trees and flowers on the landscape were strewn
Shrubs couldn't talk back to me
So I left them alone
People of my species
Were rare to come by
I saw none
Aliens all around me
I missed being home
A salty tear ran down my cheek
Droplets of sweat formed
What was my excuse this time?

I'd rather dream about love
Than actually love
The final word told.

Big Gretta

She looked normal
I never suspected a thing
She was collected
Spoke naturally
Dressed nicely
Worked efficiently
Although she had gained
A good deal of weight.
I thought nothing of it.

But when I came back
Big Gretta had died
Not a natural death
But suicide.

The self righteous
Had nagged her
Counseled her and judged her
They took her on guilt cruises
Then they had said,
"Thank God we have beautiful Christian wives
Who wouldn't think your thoughts
Let alone dare to share."
They had riddled her brain with shame
Too bad she didn't share their guile.

I toppled into my chair
When I heard the news
I was luckier than Big Gretta
And could sustain life
For one more day.

What's on your mind?

Tell me truly
What's on your mind
Looks and smiles are insufficient
Tell me you love me
Make my day
And I'll tell you I love you
Before we decay

Don't be shy
Men are supposed to be brave
I'm beginning to hate
This cat and mouse play
If you really want me
Let me know
People are wondering
When will we let go

One more time it is too late
You arrived early and couldn't wait
Where were you when I needed you?
You complain
I reply I was dreaming of you
For to dream is all I can do.

The color of the tide

High tide, low tide
Everything will be all right
People come and people go
All is well tonight
Pick me up at eight
Let us go on a date
And wish we were with the one we love to hate
Take me home, it is midnight
I regret what I ate
Tell me a kind word
When we're at the crossroads
Maybe I'll learn
How to create
A loving atmosphere
But it's too late

Remember me when I die

Jot down a tear
Make a witty remark
He is gone now
Paired off in Eden's park
Ask me a question
Then put an exclamation mark
I'll tell you the answer
At dawn in the park
Twenty five years from now
When I learn the answer
By meditating in the dark

Draw a big smile
Make it pearly white
He is gone now
It doesn't matter how.
Whether I go or stay
Part of me will pray
A soul on its knees
Regardless what the mouth may say.

Carrying on

When all I needed was a little love,
all you did was rebuff
When all I needed was compassion,
you thought it was passion
To talk, to listen
was my obsession
I guess you were not my provision

Trying to exit the west
I tried to fit in the east
I gambled with my soul
which was the wrong decision
Life and death seemed equally to be my mission

The injury of the body
is more merciful
than the soul's confusion
and as I look ahead
I wonder
Will I ever find love
beyond the barriers of communication?

Rosa

You were my only consolation
My earthly refuge.
I was beyond help
Yet you helped me.
I was beyond submission
to the dark powers
You snatched me away from them
To move, to run, became my mission
In your gentle way you said,
"That is not a solution"
You got angry
You got furious
Yet you never lost hope
of getting a glimpse of a reaction
from a dead person.

Spring always comes

In a dark room
Two beds lie side by side
A mother and her daughter lie ill
The sound of a battery operated radio
Their only cheer

Raindrops hit the window
Spring will be here soon
Muttered the mother

A new Arabic song was playing
Broadcast for the first time
Will you come split the moon with me?
Asked the singer of his love
And the mother echoed the same to her daughter
In the dimly lit room
Where mother and daughter lay ill
Yes! Spring was coming soon.

Come get bored with me

Some people cannot afford to make mistakes
It is a lifetime ordeal trying to correct them.
When you go back and retrace your steps,
you are likely to make new mistakes,
treading the familiar path, with new ways to stumble.
The old mistakes will not be repeated
New mistakes will emerge.
Please start over again
Don't try to correct the path of the past
Live the bitter, live the sweet
Cool off in the shade.
Come get bored with me
Let me offer you a chair
But wait,
When two people are together, yet lonely
The feelings of loneliness are compounded
Every eye contact reminds you of your state
And the dagger digs deeper in your heart
If you are not with someone
You have hope
that things will change
Nevertheless, we can chat away
We can think aloud
We can discover something nice to say to one another
We might get bored
But we won't make new mistakes.

The expert

She didn't mention it to me at all
I being her friend and all
She just said she didn't want to see him
And that it seemed that he wasn't as educated
as he claimed to be
after all.

She went on to take a vacation
And forgot him on
the beaches of Côte d'Azur
She simply showed up one day
bronzed and self assured as ever
Cheerful and bent on attracting another suitor.

When he tried to attract me
I was flattered, clueless as to what had happened
I let him lead me into his witty character
Unexpected things happened
And I realized I was no match for power
I fled to nurse
the self-inflicted wound

It was a decade later
That my mom
Who had insight
and saw things I did not see
Said "Your girlfriend was no friend at all,
She did not warn you
Regarding her own falter."

Background: The war in Lebanon

Labels

They call us the mentally ill,
Crazy if you will

Peace to you my crazy friends
You can vent now!

The affluent sent their sons
and daughters abroad
We were left to brood
In cold and dark corners
of make believe shelters.
We became ill against our will.

The liars lied and slept
with clear consciences
congratulating themselves
on their cleverness

                We could not lie
                But if we did
                Our souls' hearts would be left cold and bare
                Against the night's deep stare
                Naked souls in the dark
                aching with guilt
                A fertile ground
                for mental illness to breed

The thieves stole from each other
Slept soundly contemplating
tomorrow's loot

continued

> We could not steal
> But if we did
> Our souls' hearts would bleed
> Not blood
> Some kind of plasma is gushing out
> A mixture of sweat from guilt
> Tears of fear
> Racing
>   tears tired, tears resting.

The gunmen bombed us
Some muscular, some wan
Striving to vindicate
their souls' emptiness in vain
Expressing the rage of seasons without grain
Then they surrendered to deep slumber
contemplating under whose reign
will they be
come tomorrow
And on whom will they
vent their hate.

> We could never shoot
> Not if they forced us
> Never cannot follow us.

The whores sensed trouble brewing
They heard the crashes of the liars, thieves and murderers
They locked their doors out of fear
and pondered.

The predator molested the child
The whores were off duty that day
He told her he loved her
and she went his way
" I brought it on myself", she said
and ran away.

The predator slept soundly,
his mission accomplished,
Disregarding the thunder of fire.

The girl wept silently
lest someone hear

The whores opened the doors
A sound like autumn leaves wailing was heard
It was a little girl crying.

The Book and a sewing machine

The Book traveled with her
wherever she went
I took her Book with me
But her sewing machine
stayed somewhere in Beirut

When she couldn't read anymore
Kind angels read The Book
to her
When she couldn't sew anymore
Her stoic sister made her
easy to wear nightgowns
The sewing machine knew the gowns
were meant for its owner
It added a thread of love
to each stitch.

Her diligent hands stopped working
Though the perceiving eyes of her soul
saw more of life
than they ever did.

The sewing machine
dreamt of its owner's
chubby,
overworked hands
She had dismantled her machine
so many times
to ship it to her new place
They had spent so many
lamp-lit nights together
Her slim right foot on the pedal
Her busy hands adjusting the material now
Stopping the machine
then urging it on.

She made me a dress one summer night
I had to go to a Christian convention the next day
As I slept
She stayed awake sewing
chatting the night away
with old Mrs. Ovsanna,
our kindly neighbor
Easing the burden
of the labor of love.

The dress was turquoise
She had drawn the pattern of the dress herself
As she drew
the pattern of my life.

She made a golden goose
Using the sewing machine
That too was a one-night project
Her students were to perform the play
of the golden goose that lay
She drew the pattern of the goose
cut it, sewed it, stuffed it
and was at school
at her usual early hour

She drew more than patterns
She sketched lives
using The Book,
her creativity,
other books,
and a sewing machine.

Night-Sky Flyer

Just like MacNeice's westward bound train was empty*

The Olympic Airlines plane

carrying me with my two way ticket

was literally empty, but for a few energetic hostesses.

Three in the morning

We left Beirut

I waved goodbye in my heart

to a human star

that would never shine again in my life

I knew it. She knew it.

She shone in my life for thirty-two years. The end.

I have never seen such an empty goodbye.

We didn't kiss, hug, cry, or show emotion

Numb, I stood by her bed, asked her my final question

Then went into the night.

We parted forever.

The two-way ticket was just a formality.

*MacNiece's poem: Star-Gazer.

Ara
In Memoriam

Son of my brother
My favorite brother's son
Now that you're gone
I'll allow myself to brag
and sing your praises
But first, let me try
to make sense of
why you've gone.

I look for answers
I explore the Bible's depths
Come up for a short breath
then reread the book of Job
Searching for clues about patience
to cool down the embers
Embedded deep in each of our
rib cages.

Then I read what Sartre had to say
I search for words of human wisdom
Having read all, I come back to Christ
My mainstay and yours
Forgive us our trespasses I say
and to God I pray.

Born in the joy of love
Raised in bubbles of tenderness and sternness
To be buried on that hot August day
In an earthen bed
extending its arms to what lies ahead

Sweet Ara
I recall your childhood of fun
Of calling a donkey
a bird
Of lighting candles
during every Beirut blackout
And singing endless Happy Birthdays
Of quiet walks on the beach
In sunny Cyprus
Holding hands
counting sand.

I cannot forget our discussions
When you became of age
about the kingdom
And God's only begotten Son
Even across the miles
We could feel your smile
that cheered us
and lifted our spirits
when life dragged them down.

You were bright and quick
as light
Stubborn in your faith as a bull
In a fight
You were gentle and comforting
like the morning mist
after a long, hot night.
Your sense of humor and transparency
transcended your years
and in your hurry
to pack for eternity's best
You forgot to live your life here
On this tired planet.

The Falafel Shop

Falafel is my favorite food. It is a Middle Eastern food comparable to vegetarian burgers here in America. I know that it is deep fried in very high temperature oil. People usually eat it in sandwich form rolled inside pita bread, opened to form a delicious pocket that holds the falafel pieces.

There is a falafel shop in Beirut called Falafel Arax. A short skinny man used to fry the falafel. He is probably there right now and I can imagine him in a white, spotless T-shirt frying falafel from mid-morning until late at night. He has a meek expression. His feet are firmly planted in the little shop. Day after day, he stands behind the huge deep frying dish. I do not know his name. Let us call him Saro.

When I obtained my Lebanese Baccalaureate Part II, I celebrated with a falafel sandwich fried by Saro. When I received my Bachelor's degree, I took home a few falafel sandwiches to celebrate with my mother. I still did not have a job, and since I loved education, I was encouraged to obtain my Master's degree. Was falafel due on this occasion too?

Saro, the dedicated falafel fryer is still there. There was war in Lebanon so I searched the world for a safe place to stay. In my search, I changed cities and countries. I worked and frequently changed jobs because when I was bored with a job, I felt that I was suffocating in that workplace. I had an unknown dream but I knew that if I saw my dream career I would recognize it. Moving became a habit, but I was not happy with where I lived nor with the offices I held. All my life I had wanted to live in America. I always believed that I would belong there. When my dream of coming to America and actualizing myself came true, I was elated. Falafel was due on this happy occasion.

As far as my career, even here in America, I never found a job that really made me happy. The allure of any position soon passed away, and I found myself searching for a dream one more time. Greatly disillusioned and tired from too many dreams and too many ambitions I returned to visit Beirut. I passed by Falafel Arax in 2007. Saro was there quietly frying falafel. I stared at him. I wondered what Saro's secret of accepting his lot in life was. Don't tell me he was happy with his job. I could read the expression of smugness and disgust in his eyes every time I have seen him. But he hung in there for many years. What is your secret Saro?

Disappointments

When disappointment after disappointment comes my way
I remind myself that Christ is the way
Doubts churn in my heart and brain
Gossip abounds
I advise myself when alone
Wear your courage like a coat
go in the cold
Don't tolerate thoughts of misfortune
from days of old
There is no room for harboring regrets
not from the past
nor the present
or ever.

Some lives cramp so many mistakes
In such a short period of time
opportunities dim to no longer rise
It becomes a game of survival
where mistakes are fatal

Then I open the Bible
Things deemed impossible become possible
Mistakes are forgotten
New beginnings are free
Even life eternal
for the mortal.

The Bug

Go home bug!
I do not want to squish you
under my sole.
Some people claim that you do,
and I have always wondered if
you have a soul.

You seem to wander aimlessly
But all creatures have a purpose
Go find your luck elsewhere
and good luck in your endeavors
Who am I to end your
pre-determined life-cycle
with a twist of my ankle?

Go home bug!
Now, now
Don't make me commit a crime
under the crescent moon!
I just came out here to light a cigarette.
Your ancestors possibly lived here
long before I moved in.
Your nest must be in the back yard
You are some bug's mom
some other insect's or bird's main meal
Don't make me disturb nature's course
Go about your own business
and leave me alone
to appreciate my cigarette
and to think about a man
far, far away
who told me when I tried to get in touch with him
"I don't want to bug you."

Let it take its course

When it comes
Don't try to stop it
Don't try to further its course
Let it take its time
Don't meddle
It will fall
when it is time for it to fall

It will start by a few drops at first
A hint, an agreement, a recognition
It might pour
It might not
If it does
You'll see a wetting of the pavements of your heart
Then puddles will form
Beware of driving by the puddles!
You might splash a saint
and chase him away

Sweet, fresh, and inviting
a river forms in the depths of your heart
The river slowly carves a path
Weeds may start growing
Be careful. Pull the weeds!
Cultivate the land by the river
and you'll have your own choice
of what grows on the banks of
the river in your heart.

Celebration of Armenian Tradition
"Shoorch Bar"
(Circle Dance)

Dance to the rhythm
Set your body free
Dance to the music
Go on a dancing spree
Relax
You're at home
In a large Armenian family
Be carefree.

Round and round they went
The older men went by the slower rhythm
The younger ones went fast
The older women
hooked their little fingers together
And swayed their souls to the ancient Armenian melodies.
Some parents and grandparents
proudly held their babies
and rocked with them
to the lively music.
The younger girls hopped along
Leading all the dancers in the vast hall
between tables and chairs
Filled with men, women, and children
clapping, talking, eating and drinking
listening and enjoying
reliving memories of what might have been
in a land that's everyone's dream.

continued

The musicians young and old
Playing the kamancha, oud, and kanum
the duduk and the dumbeg
created an enchanted mood.
The beat grew louder
Spirits were lifted higher
The hall turned into a mass of people
United in their quest
(Whether or not they managed the right steps)
To breathe life into old Armenian folklore
with the spirit emerging from ancient
happy melodies of Armenia.

Jano

Soul mate of mine
The one who comes to me
As a result of work divine
The one who tries to understand
what no one else would
of past, present, and future plans.
How can time ever erase
all your kindness and grace?
They are etched in my brain
and in my heart's deepest place.

What can I say to make you happy?
Not a poem, not a story born during the night
But a well kept house
is your idea of an accomplished spouse.
From now on, I promise to be
as quiet as a mouse
while you sleep and I write
Good night!

The prodigal daughter

Don't search for happiness
In estranged places
It will come when it comes
You come home now
Wait for it at home
where you are welcome truly,
and not out of courtesy.

Come home now
We will make a life for you here
Be safe. Be warm. Sleep tight
I will chase away the crazed roosters
That dare wake you up.
I will chase the owls, the bats
and all the rats.
No one can hurt you here
Home is safe
and the sun shines for you
every night in my heart
I will protect you from the bombs.
You know,
There are worse things than war
Home is home even if there's war outside.
Mansions in peaceful lands
Or lonely apartments of sand
In desolate yet rich places,
can sometimes do more harm
than men with grenades.

There are no lighthouses in foreign lands
Come home
Two can live as cheaply as one
Forget life's strife
Come home to my open heart
and dwell forever inside.

Honey's honey

My Honey's honey
is made in the breeze
The olive trees dance freely
The figs ripen and fall
The birds carry the nectar
and drop it in mid-flight
to the cruising bees
Freely, freely in the breeze.

My Honey's honey
is sweeter than droplets
of water
absorbed by parched land
Sweeter than dew in the morning land
perfumed with incense
and orange blossom oil
People only wish to have it
But they can't.

My Honey's honey is sweeter than money
for money changes hands
I store my honey's honey
in a pot of gold,
along with old works of art,
special Christmas cards,
epistles of madmen, and
my daydreams and thoughts,
that no one can behold
and only heaven understands.

Where am I from?

I am from the mountains and the seaside
I am from the countryside and the city
I am from the ghetto and better neighborhoods
I am from bloodshed, guns, bombs and grenades
I am from the cypress trees and the majestic cedars
I am from the ancient castles and modern buildings
I am from palaces and extravagance
I am from an outdoor museum
I am from the rivers and pebbles
I am from Shawarma and Hummos
I am from a cactus plant playing the role of a Christmas tree
I am from palm leaves and candles
I am from bread and cheese
I am from lavender and honeybees
But, most of all, I am from blessings
And living in His infinite grace.

The Ripple Prayer

Dear God
Forgive me for all my sins
Whether in thought or deed
Forgive me for the rational and irrational thoughts
Forgive me for my conscious and sub-conscious dreams
Take my hand
and lead me in Your ways
Forgive me
For loving some human beings more than You
For remembering them more than I remember You
For seeking their company more than I seek Yours
Remind me to thank you for my family and friends
Who are Your creation
Humbly teach me to accept misfortune
and good fortune
as consequences of human life.
Bless my family and friends
and their families and friends
Let your blessings flow
like ripples
blessing all humanity
through the ripple prayer.

Printed in the United States
222158BV00002B/2/P